THIS IS THE STORY OF BILLY'S SEARCH FOR PIRATE TREASURE, UNDER THE SEA.

On his quest he makes friends with the fish and receives a liberal education in marine life. He meets "Nosey," the black-and-gold Angel Fish, he has a little Sea Horse for a guide and rides on a Green Sea Turtle. The fish all have individual personalities, and Billy talks with them.

My idea for this story started years ago, when my husband and I operated a glass-bottom boat which made it possible to see a small part of this fantastic undersea world. We used to say: "Wouldn't it be wonderful if we could swim and breathe in this undersea fairyland like the fish?"

I believe my son, Russell, who illustrated the story, is part *fish*, since he spends so much time under water … he really *could* be Billy of the story.

I hope you will enjoy your swim with Billy on his undersea adventure and learn about another world. Maybe you will find some treasure — the old Green Sea Turtle knows the secret!

Minerva J. Smiley

Billy's Search for

Florida
undersea
Treasure

A STORY BY MINERVA J. SMILEY
ILLUSTRATED BY RUSS SMILEY

STORY BY MINERVA J. SMILEY
DESIGNED AND ILLUSTRATED BY RUSS SMILEY

Copyright 2002 Russ Smiley

ISBN: 0-89317-047-X

Published by

Windward Publishing

3943 Meadowbrook Road
Minneapolis, MN 55426-4505
A DIVISION OF FINNEY COMPANY

Printed in Canada

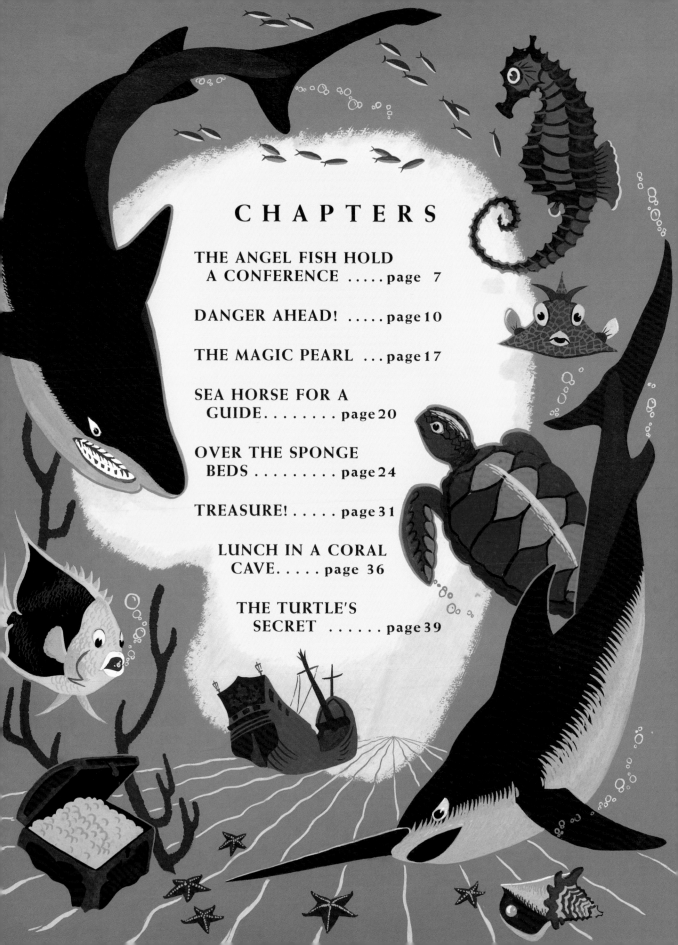

CHAPTERS

THE ANGEL FISH
HOLD A CONFERENCE

IN A BLUE TROPIC SEA, under a sunlit coral ledge, the black-and-gold Angel Fish were holding a conference.

"Impossible!" snapped the Queen Angel Fish, fanning herself with her yellow fins. "Who is this boy? What is he doing swimming under water? Why does he want to find that old sunken Galleon? Why should we tell him where to find the magic pearl?"

"Go on, answer me," said the Queen to one little black-and-gold Angel Fish who swam out from under a purple sea plume.

"Well, Queen, I like him and I want to help him."

"I know, I know" answered the Queen. "You have told me all that before."

"The Queen is absolutely right," spoke up the King, swimming quietly into view. "Furthermore, little Angel Fish, I have been told about your following this boy around just like he was another fish."

"Oh! I suppose those gossipy parrot fish told you. I wish they would stay home in the coral forest where they belong."

"Never mind about the parrot fish, continue your story about this boy."

"Yes, sir, his name is Billy and he calls me Nosey."

"Nosey! Ha, Ha," laughed the King Angel Fish, "a good name, and you will no doubt 'nosey' yourself into a lot of trouble, but go on with your story."

"Billy lives with his father and mother on that large sail boat anchored off Key Largo. He wears a tank on his back that makes bubbles — he told me this is how he carries his air supply. He really looks funny with flappy fins on his feet and a glass mask that covers his eyes and nose; but he can stay under water a long time and swims quite well."

"One day Billy was exploring in Angel Fish Creek and I nibbled his fingers real hard and said, 'Hi! Why don't you talk to me?' My, was he surprised! Now I meet Billy every day and we talk and he tells me lots of secrets."

"Secrets, secrets, what *are* they?" asked the King.

"Billy has just one big secret, which is to find an old pirate treasure chest filled with gold and silver coins, pearls, rubies, emeralds, jade and ..."

"Stop! Gracious me, is that all he wants?" asked the Queen, blinking her opal eyes. "Just how does Billy expect to find this treasure chest?"

"Billy says that hundreds of years ago, pirates sunk many ships off the Florida coast and there's lots of treasure left in the hulls of old sunken Galleons."

"That all may be true," answered the King, "but why should we be interested?"

"Oh, we are going to help him! I told Billy about the ship the old Green Sea Turtle is always spinning yarns about, and now I want to help him find the safest and shortest way to get there."

"Stuff and nonsense," answered the King, "there is no safe or short way to reach that old Galleon, and a human swimming around in the ocean would probably look very attractive to a barracuda, or a shark. A nice dinner he would make for some hungry fish."

"H'm," continued the King, "so you have already told Billy about the Green Sea Turtle, who knows all the secrets of the sea and also where to find the magic pearl?"

"Well, no, I haven't," answered Nosey, "not everything. I told Billy I could not help him anymore until I had your permission to do so."

"Well, Queen, what do you think we should do about this?"

"I've been thinking, King, that Billy can never find that sunken ship without our help and that of other friendly fish. Perhaps if Nosey took Billy on a journey through our beautiful undersea gardens, he would give up that dangerous adventure."

"Oh dear me," said Nosey, "such a fuss; it's only an old pirate chest that Billy wants to find. Please let me help him."

"All right, all right," answered the Queen, "swim along now to Billy's boat and tell him you can help … and go with him to the edge of the coral reef. From there on he will be on his own."

"OK, King and Queen, and I thank you both very much." And Nosey swam away toward Billy's boat.

DANGER AHEAD!

THE FLORIDA SUN was warm, and a soft tropic breeze blew through the sail of Billy's boat. "Oh, dear me!" thought Billy, "I'm getting sleepier and sleepier every minute."

Then glancing over the edge of the boat he saw Nosey swimming toward him. So he slipped his lung, mask and flippers on and eased into the water.

"Boy! am I glad to see you, Nosey! Tell me quick, do you have good news from the King and Queen of the black-and-gold Angel Fish?"

"Both the King and Queen think you should give up your quest, but they did say I could take you on a trip through our undersea gardens… and then, if you still wish to continue your treasure hunt, you can go on your own. I can help you only as far as the coral reef and then I must return to my home in the coral cave."

"Sounds like fun. Come on, Nosey, let's get started."

As they swam along in the clear blue water, Billy said, "Oh, this is really super, just like wrapping yourself in soft blue clouds and flying over a colorful flower garden." A garden of royal purple plumes, just like ostrich feathers, and lacy waving fans in pink and yellow; even a forest of white coral trees, through which swam tropical fish gayer in color than the brightest birds of the jungle.

They swam right into a school of dolphins, hundreds of them, their scales of blue and yellow glittering like jewels as they swam along.

"Nosey, look beneath us, there are stars, hundreds of stars. I never expected to see stars walking around on the floor of the ocean!"

"Those are star fish, Billy; they are little animals and very much alive. See the five perfect points, just like a real star? The little prongs or points that stick out all over them are what they walk with. In the center is a mouth which is also a stomach. They glide over the food they want, and suck it in … and I tell you, Billy, the oyster families don't like star fish; they are about the only animal in the ocean that can make an oyster open its shell."

"Really, how come?" asked Billy.

"They just glide quietly over the oyster's shell until they get it right in the center under them, then they bend down the five points of the star around it, squeeze just the right spot — and bing! The shell opens and the oyster goes into the mouth of the star fish."

"Look! look!" said Nosey, "under that stag-horn coral tree. See all those striped yellow and black fish. They are called prison fish — most likely because of the yellow and black stripes, and they always swim in gangs. But I must say they look very happy.

"They should be happy in such a wonderful prison," replied Billy.

"The yellow and pink plants you see over there are called sea fans because they are always waving and curling around with the tide, but the funny part of it is, they are not plants at all."

"Then what in the world are they?" asked Billy.

"Why, they are colonies or families of small animals. They grow on a solid coral base which makes them look like plants. Most everything down here in the ocean is an animal of some kind. Look over there at that coral. There are many different kinds of coral, in all sorts of fantastic shapes and sizes. Right over there is a piece of brain coral, shaped in little scrolls like a man's brain is supposed to be. That delicate coral white and finely patterned is lace coral. This coral hangs like the softest knitted lace on the plants at the bottom of the ocean. Some coral is formed like the propeller on a boat, others like a giant's tooth."

"It takes hundreds and hundreds of years for coral to grow. Every little curlycue and fancy scroll design was once a little live animal or polyp. These little animals get lime and phosphate from the water, with which they make coral houses, and they keep on building and living and dying in these houses on through the ages."

Just then … Nosey suddenly darted to one side.

"Why the detour?" yelled Billy.

"Just a jelly fish. I always give them plenty of room to pass by."

"Seems silly to swim away from a jelly fish. I think they look very pretty, drifting along like an umbrella."

"That's *your* opinion," answered Nosey, "but those jelly fish have wicked sting cells which give them the power to sting small fish for food. They also sting the mouths of larger fish. I know from experience."

"My! it's an unusual world down here," said Billy, as they continued their journey, "and this is all very interesting … but do you know, Nosey, I still want to find the sunken Galleon and a treasure chest."

"Yes, I know, Billy, but forget it for now, we are swimming to the edge of a reef and should see a lot of fish."

Sure enough, they swam into a school of blue fish, their scales flashing like an "Alice Blue Gown" in the clear ocean light.

As they swam over a coral ledge, two blue-and-gold Angel Fish nodded to Nosey and slyly winked at Billy. As they disappeared in a mist of bubbles, a large school of grunts passed by (little fish that really *do* make a grunting sound)! These were followed by silver mullet, yellow tail, snapper, spade fish, blue runners and butterfly fish.

"Goodness me!" exclaimed Billy. "It's a regular fish parade. This is exciting!"

"Yes, too exciting," answered Nosey. "Something's up. I feel danger, so stay close to me and swim quickly to that overhanging coral ledge ahead."

"Golly! what's going on, Nosey? I hear a rushing, swishing sound. What is it?"

"Never mind, just keep swimming as fast as you can — we have to get to the coral ledge."

And not a minute too soon. From above they heard a lashing noise, then there was a lunge of foam and bubbles, and a long slick gray body streaked by, slashing into a school of Spanish mackerel.

"Wow! a *shark!* Did you see that look in his eye, Nosey?"

"I sure did — but we are safe now, Billy."

"Say, did you know that sharks have seven rows of teeth, and wink their eyes to and fro like a shower curtain?"

"Don't want one winking at *me*, anytime! I'm sure glad he's gone."

"I've been thinking, Billy — it might be wise for you to take the King's and Queen's advice and give up your search. Sharkey's parting look could mean trouble."

"Yes, I know, Nosey, but I still want to find that treasure chest. But don't think I'm not enjoying this undersea journey with you. It's all so colorful and bright down here — reminds me of pictures in a book, only this is better because it's always changing. Yet I think I've had enough of coral plants that are really animals. What about the magic pearl you told me about?"

"All right, Billy," answered Nosey. "I guess you are still determined to take that dangerous journey. Soon we will be over a stretch of sandy bottom that will lead us to the home of the conch shells."

THE MAGIC PEARL

AS THEY SWAM ALONG, Nosey said, "Did I ever tell you, Billy, how I found out about the magic pearl?"

"No, you didn't. How did you find out?"

"Well, Billy, the old Green Sea Turtle told me that many, many years ago a King and Queen Conch made themselves a nice cozy home, deep in a sand bar on the floor of the ocean.

"Then one day a large boat anchored over the sand bar, and a diver dove down to the floor of the ocean looking for conch shells. He found the King Conch, pulled it up from its sandy home, and took it back to his boat.

"Of course, with her King gone, the Queen was very sad and lonesome. So, as the story goes, early one morning she rose to the surface of the ocean, to see if she could see the boat that had carried away her King. The boat was gone — and the tears the Queen shed froze into a pearl. The pearl caught the pink color of any early-morning sunbeam, and was made magic by a little sea spirit floating down the sunbeam.

"And here we are NOW! over the bed of the conch shells, hundreds of them. But Billy, before you start looking for this magic pearl, remember you will find it only in the rose-pink lips of the Queen. The lips of the King Conch are a golden speckled brown."

"H'm," mused Billy. "You mean to tell me, Nosey, that out of all these shells I must find the Queen Conch that has the pink magic pearl?"

"Right you are, Billy, so get started. Keep turning those shells."

Billy worked and worked. But all the shells he turned over were King Conchs, and he was getting very, very tired.

"Oh dear!" said Billy, "I must rest a minute."

So he swam over to a coral head; then in looking around he noticed, against a purple coral tree, the tip peak of an unusually large shell.

"Well," thought Billy, "won't hurt to investigate … maybe the Queen is still grieving and is hiding away from the other shells."

So with Nosey close behind him, he swam over and discovered a shell partly covered with sand. The conch did not want to be disturbed, but Billy dug and dug and pulled and pulled, and at last was able to get it up and turn it over.

"Oh, boy!" exclaimed Billy, as before his startled eyes rolled a pearl making a brilliant spot of pink in the dim blue ocean light.

"Quick, Billy," said Nosey, "pick it up — that's the *magic* pearl!"

"I know, but I'm almost afraid to pick it up. Just think — a magic pearl. Come on, Nosey, let's be on our way to the ship."

"Not so fast, Billy, we will soon be nearing the coral reef, where I must leave you. Remember now, don't lose the magic pearl, because the little sea spirit that guards it may save your life if you encounter danger. Oh, one more thing before I leave you — be sure and watch for the little Sea Horse, at the end of the coral trees. He will act as your guide if he takes a liking to you."

"I'll be watching for him, and thank you very much for everything," answered Billy, waving good-bye to his friend, the little Angel Fish.

SEA HORSE FOR A GUIDE

BILLY WAS VERY LONESOME and frightened after leaving Nosey. But holding the magic pearl tightly in his hand, he swam on through the coral trees. Then he noticed, a short distance ahead through the branches of the white and purple trees, the parrot fish that Nosey had told him about.

Swimming over to them, he said, "Hello, Mrs. Parrot Fish. My! you *are* a brilliant colored fish. I bet the parrots of the jungle don't have feathers as bright as your green scales."

"Well, never having seen a parrot of the jungle or any other kind of bird, I wouldn't know, but I'm satisfied. And that was a very pretty speech you made," chuckled Mrs. Parrot Fish.

"Ha, ha," laughed another parrot fish swimming by, "pretty speech, pretty speech."

Suddenly Mrs. Parrot Fish frowned and said, "Go on, little boy, you can't fool me with your funny face and fish tails on your feet. What are you doing down here in the ocean?"

"Gee, Mrs. Parrot Fish, you're very curious."

"Curious, curious, did you say?"

"Please, Mrs. Parrot Fish, don't swim away. I was just going to ask you the way to the old sunken Galleon. Perhaps you will help me."

"Billy, Billy, if you take my advice you will turn around and swim back to shore and safety. Here on the coral reef the fish are friendly, but before you reach that old Galleon, you will have to swim over sponge beds and sandy bottom, with not one tiny place to hide from big fish."

"Yes, I suppose you are right. I have been warned by the King and Queen of the Angel Fish and my friend Nosey, too — but I will succeed if you and the other fish will help me."

"Not much I can do, Billy, the old Green Sea Turtle is the only one in the sea that knows about sunken Galleons and lost treasure. So I certainly hope you meet her somewhere on your journey."

"I hope so too," answered Billy, "it's been nice seeing you and I hope we meet again."

"We may, we may," chorused the parrot fish, as Billy waved good-bye and swam on through the coral trees.

"Dear me!," thought Billy, "I must keep a sharp lookout for the little Sea Horse, I would hate to miss him."

Just as he reached the end of the coral forest, he heard a little voice say, "Hi! Billy, here I am."

"Looking around he saw the Sea Horse. He was balancing to and fro with his tail curled around the branch of a coral tree.

"Oh, there you are," said Billy, "I'm sure glad to see you, little Sea Horse."

"You *should* be glad, you almost missed me! But I was watching for you — so come on, Billy, let's be on our way." The Sea Horse giggled and said, "You are a funny sight in that outfit."

"Yes, I know, but it's nice to have company. Where do you suggest we go from here, Sea Horse?"

"I know a Cow Fish that lives on a grassy plain not far from here; she may have some useful information. Look! there she is now. You swim over and talk to her, Billy, I'll stay close by and listen."

"Good morning, Cow Fish," said Billy.

"Good morning yourself. What can I do for you?" asked the Cow Fish.

"I thought perhaps you could tell me the quickest way to reach the old Galleon."

"Well, Billy, I seldom leave my grassy plain, but I was talking to some Nassau Grouper passing this way. They had heard all about you and said to tell you, if you passed by, that the sunken Galleon is not too near and not too far."

"Ho, ho," laughed the Sea Horse, "that information is not much help."

As Billy and the Sea Horse swam further and further from the safety of the coral forest, the ocean floor seemed to grow bigger and bigger. In the distance it looked like a desert of drifting sand. Hundreds of fish swam by, but they only glanced at Billy and the Sea Horse with an indifferent stare.

"Look!" said the Sea Horse. "Do you see that happy-looking fish swimming toward us? It's a jolly Jew Fish. You might hail him and find out if *he* has ever visited the *old wreck*."

"Good idea," answered Billy.

So swimming toward him, Billy called, "Hi there, Jew Fish, please stop and talk to me and tell me about the *old Galleon*. Have you ever been there?"

"Oh, yes, yes," replied the Jew Fish. "I have been there many times. I enjoy eating the crabs and lobster that live on the bottom of *that old ship*. They are delicious … but you don't look hungry. Why do you want to find *that old boat*?"

"Well, it's this way. I want to go inside the ship and see if the pirates left just one treasure chest."

"Sounds interesting, Billy, and I wish you luck. Swim over the sponge beds, then swim east, and it won't be long before you will see the dim outline of *the old ship*."

OVER THE SPONGE BEDS

So Billy and the little Sea Horse continued their journey. "We'll keep close to the sandy bottom," said the Sea Horse, "where there is less danger of attracting big fish."

They were so busy talking, they were swimming over the sponge beds before they realized it.

"This is nice," said Billy, "everything so quiet and peaceful with the warm sunshine coming through the blue water. Pshaw! Who's afraid to swim over the sponge beds? Seems silly, all the warning from the fishes about sponge beds."

"Don't be too sure," warned the Sea Horse, "we are not over them yet, remember!"

How true, for at that moment the Sea Horse heard a distant commotion. His ears went backwards and forwards and his eyes rolled in alarm. A splashing was coming near and nearer. Hundreds of small fish swam by with lightning speed.

"Oh, dear me!" said the Sea Horse, "it's a big Barracuda, known as the Tiger of the Sea."

"Barracuda, did you say?" shouted Billy. "Oh, where can we go? Can't we dive down and hide under one of those big sponges?"

"No, no, there isn't time. He is almost over us. Billy, Billy, don't be so stupid. Use your magic pearl."

"Help! Help!" screamed Billy, "Help! Help!"

Magically and suddenly a black curtain dropped. Blacker and blacker became the water. Not a ray of light came through.

"Little Sea Horse, where are you?" called Billy. "Don't leave me."

"I'm here and still breathing. Don't be frightened, Billy, the ink fish came to our rescue. They shot black clouds of ink just as the Barracuda had decided to make a dive at us. Of course he couldn't find us in the dark, so he swam away."

"Lucky me. Boy, oh boy! I sure was scared."

"Lucky me too," said the Sea Horse, "but next time you are in danger, don't be so slow or so dumb. I'm not anxious to find myself in the belly of a fish."

"I have heard that Barracudas don't bite people — they are just curious. He may have been after those blue runners that swam by, but curious or not, I don't trust him."

"That goes for me, too, little Sea Horse. I can still see that Barracuda's big mouth with those long four-inch teeth, and I am still shivering."

"Well, stop shivering and look straight ahead."

Billy blinked and blinked but couldn't believe what he saw. "Oh, it can't be true!" thought Billy, "it just isn't real."

But it was true. The outlines of the old Galleon were just faintly visible through the distant blue water.

"Come on, come on, little Sea Horse, I can hardly wait to get there!"

"Don't rush, Billy, it's quite a swim, so take it cautiously, there might be more danger ahead."

So Billy and the Sea Horse set a direct course, never losing sight of the distant ship. The sponge beds were far behind them. They were swimming over smooth sandy bottom, with scattered coral trees, and waving plumes and sea fans.

Both Billy and the little Sea Horse were so intent on reaching the Galleon, they had failed to notice the dark gray shadows hovering over the old ship. When they did look up, the shadows had taken form and were coming closer and closer.

Then to their horror and fright, they realized they were sharks, which were swimming directly toward them.

"Oh, little Sea Horse," exclaimed Billy, what will we *do?*"

"Courage, Billy, maybe they haven't spied us yet. If we can only make it to the hull of the ship, we can hide and be safe."

"I don't think I can swim any faster, little Sea Horse, but I'll try."

"It's too late, Billy, they see us … and here they come."

Billy looked up, and right into the cruel eyes of a shark. He seemed to smile at him with a victorious grin.

Then suddenly Billy laughed. "Ha! Ha! I'm not afraid of you. Come on and see if I care. You don't know that I have a magic pearl, but I have. Ha! Ha!"

Billy opened his mouth to call "HELP!" — but the words froze in his throat, and his heart pounded against his ribs. The magic pearl was gone … gone.

Trembling with fear, Billy watched the large fish curl around him like a banking airplane. The shark was grinning and opening his big mouth.

Billy made one desperate effort to swim and get away. "I can't give up. I have to reach the old Galleon. Don't leave me, little Sea Horse," he pleaded.

He could almost feel the teeth of the shark on him. It seemed he could not swim another stroke, when he heard the little Sea Horse say: "Billy, quick — look in the curve of my tail."

There was the magic pearl, twinkling like a tiny pink light. Billy seized it in his hand, and not a second too soon.

He faintly gasped. "Please, HELP! HELP! don't let …"

There was a loud roar and a splash, and out of a wave appeared a school of porpoise. Billy and the little Sea Horse quickly swam to one side.

The porpoise rushed in to battle the sharks. There was a great thrashing and splashing, which rose to the din of a mighty battle. The water was a big rolling swell of milky white bubbles. The porpoise were furiously butting and batting the sharks with all their might.

The sharks fought desperately to get away, but it was no use. Exhausted and beaten, they soon sank to the floor of the ocean.

"Whew," said Billy, "thanks to the porpoise, the fight is over, and I am not sorry to see the end of those sharks. Come, little Sea Horse, let's forget our troubles and swim over to the ship."

"Just a minute, Billy, you had better put the pearl back in the curve of my tail. Any more trouble and we'll know where to find it."

"All right, little Sea Horse, I'm putting it back in the curve of your tail. Thanks for finding it and saving my life."

TREASURE!

BILLY and the little Sea Horse swam only a short distance when they found themselves in the shadow of the hull of that old old Galleon.

"Boy, oh boy!" exclaimed Billy. "Just think — 'Once upon a Time' this old Galleon was a big beautiful ship! I would like to have seen her with all her rigging and big white sails. I bet it was a fierce battle before the captain of *this* ship let the pirates come aboard and rob her of all her treasure."

"No doubt about it being a big battle," answered the little Sea Horse, "but that all happened hundreds of years ago. I thought you were interested in finding out if those pirates left any treasure."

"I am ... let's swim up to the deck and find a way to get inside."

So up to the deck they swam, searching all over, in and out of broken cabins and through the spooky galley.

"Creepers!" said Billy. "It sure is dark, gloomy and dingy in here. And look at all those fish! Must be thousands of them."

Just as they decided to go down into the very bottom of the old ship, a brilliant shaft of sunlight came through an open hatchway, forming a rainbow of colors. The light seemed to reach to a faraway corner, deep down. Billy and the Sea Horse swam through the brilliant colors and the open hatch. As they looked around they noticed sticking out of the sand an old wooden chest. It took them a few moments to get used to the dim light, but as they did so, other objects became clear — such as rotted coils of rope, iron chains, old anchors, cannon balls.

On examining the chest, they found it covered with sea weed, slimy moss and barnacles. The old hinges and lock could hardly be seen.

"What are you waiting for, Billy?" asked the Sea Horse. "It's a pirate chest, that's what you wanted to find, isn't it? Why you made this journey under the sea? Come on, open it."

"Yes, yes, I know," answered Billy. "I can hardly wait to open it. I want to see the gold and silver coins and precious jewels."

Billy scraped off the slimy moss, sea weed and barnacles and found the old rusty lock. He pulled and pulled and lifted with all his might and strength. But the lock was stuck hard and fast in the wood of the old chest. It didn't even budge.

"I've just got to open it," thought Billy. "There must be some way to get it open."

While Billy and the Sea Horse were both trying to solve the problem, who should come down the shaft of light into the hold of the ship but Mrs. Parrot Fish.

"Hello, Billy," said the Parrot Fish. "What seems to be the trouble? I was curious to see how you were getting along, so I decided to swim over from the coral forest and find out."

"I'm so glad you did," answered Billy, "I'm really having trouble; I just can't budge this old lock."

"Pshaw," answered the Parrot Fish. "No trouble at all. I can bite that lock away from the wood in no time — that's play for me. I often bite right through a fish hook, when some fisherman thinks he has me hooked."

Mrs. Parrot Fish went busily to work, and in a very few minutes the lock was free from the wood of the chest.

"There you are, Billy," said the Parrot Fish. "Now go ahead and open it. I want to look inside."

Billy grasped the lid tightly in both hands, shut his eyes, and counted, "One, two, three."

The old hinges screeched – and the lid of the chest flew open. Billy opened his eyes and looked inside. He quickly shut them and looked again and then again. No mistake. It was true! The chest was empty! Not even one silver coin or sparkling jewel.

For a moment he could not believe it. He tried to speak and couldn't. Tears burned his eyes, his heart pounded and his throat hurt.

He glanced at his friends, the Parrot Fish and the little Sea Horse, both of whom had been so good to him … and he tried to smile. Before he could say anything, all three heard a big noise overhead.

"Sounds like company," said the Sea Horse. And they all looked toward the shaft of light.

"Hello, Hello!" said a gruff voice. "What's going on down here?"

"Gee! it's the old Green Sea Turtle," exclaimed Billy.

"Hi there, Billy," said the Turtle. "Your friend Nosey, the black-and-gold Angel Fish asked me to come to this old wreck and see if you needed any help. My! My! never did I see such a glum-looking group."

"I'm truly glad to see you," answered Billy, "but I'm feeling very sad and disappointed. Look, Sea Turtle, look at this treasure chest. It's empty, just empty."

"Oh-oh, I was afraid of that," said the Turtle, "but things never are as bad as they seem … and this adventure may turn out better than you think. Later, I may tell you a secret, but right now I have a surprise for you."

"A surprise! What kind?"

"You are invited to have lunch in a coral cave. The invitation is from the King and Queen of the Angel Fish. Your friend Nosey will be there to greet you. Come on, let's get out of this gloomy old Galleon and be on our way. Climb atop my back, Billy, and I will give you a ride to the coral cave."

So waving good-bye to his friends, Mrs. Parrot Fish and the Sea Horse, Billy got on the back of the old Sea Turtle and they swam away through the clear green water.

LUNCH IN A CORAL CAVE

AFTER RIDING over the water for some distance the Sea Turtle said, "Well, Billy, feeling any better?"

"Yes, I am, thanks to you, Sea Turtle. This is a thrilling ride — but I can't help wondering about the secret."

"Oh, I know a lot of secrets about this undersea world. My family have lived in the sea for thousands and thousands of years, and have seen many sunken ships on the floor of the ocean. But we have no time for stories now, because we are already late for lunch. After lunch I will return you to your boat, and on the way tell you the big secret."

"Well, I'll admit, Sea Turtle, I haven't eaten for quite awhile; I would enjoy a lunch."

It seemed only a moment later that Billy and the Green Sea Turtle swam into a cool cave under a ledge of pink coral. The cave looked like an undersea cafe.

Surprise of surprises! Billy saw all the fish he had met on his way to the old Galleon and more, too. Such a gathering:

There were parrot fish flashing their scales of purple, red and green, and giving Billy a knowing nod. The cow fish from the grassy plain nodded and the hog fish grunted and grinned at Billy — all in a very friendly manner.

The King and Queen of the black-and-gold Angel Fish arrived, followed by Nosey. But before Billy could say, "Hi, Nosey!" a pair of dolphins waved their fins at him.

More and more fish arrived. The jolly Jew Fish, too, grinning as usual. Several red snapper swam into view, looking very snappy in their rose-pink scales. Some yellow tails came in a hurry.

The fishes lay very still and smiled a greeting to Billy.

As guest of honor Billy was invited to sit down on a large sea shell, before a white sandy table. The Green Sea Turtle swam down beside him, Nosey, the little Angel fish on the other side.

"My! My!" thought Billy, "this is truly wonderful … and the strangest party I was ever invited to."

As he gazed in amazement, his pal the little Sea Horse came into view. He swam round and round a rose coral centerpiece, then perched on top of the flower of stone and saucily bowed to Billy.

The feast began with coquina soup served in golden-brown conch shells. The Green Sea Turtle handed Billy a yellow sea-fan plate filled with fat pink shrimp.

"Yum, yum," said Billy, "these are the best shrimp I ever tasted." Then he opened a small, ridged, fan-shaped shell and decided they tasted just like clams he had eaten at home, only better, so cool and sweet and a tiny bit salty.

"Hey, Billy," called a starfish, "you aren't eating your oysters. Don't you like them?"

"Not very much; I will leave them for you."

At this moment a gang of prison fish, in their black and yellow stripes, swam into view. As Billy followed their gaze he saw a large sea-fan platter of stone crabs and crawfish tails. Beside the platter were sea eggs with the quills removed. And on a coral lace doily were snowy white sea biscuits. The feast ended with a dessert of round chocolate sea beans.

"Never, never," said Billy, "will I forget this party under the sea, with all the fishes and such good things to eat!"

"Yes, it has been nice, but it must end," said the old Green Sea Turtle. "Come on, Billy we must be on our way back to your boat."

So Billy waved good-bye to all the fishes, with a special wave to Nosey, Mrs. Parrot Fish, and the little Sea Horse.

"Hurry, Billy, jump on my back and hold tight." Around the Turtle's neck went Billy's arms. And did that Turtle swim! Objects and fish of all kinds and colors passed by with magic speed.

THE TURTLE'S SECRET

AFTER BILLY and the Turtle had been swimming atop the green water for some distance, Billy said, "Will you tell me the secret? I can hardly wait to hear it."

"Now, now, don't rush me. You will hear it all in good time," answered the Turtle. "It's a long story and it may be hard for you to believe, but it's true."

"A long, long time ago, I saw that old Galleon you were on today … at a time when she was a full-rigged beautiful ship carrying valuable cargo from Spain to Cuba. On one of her sailing trips through these very waters, she was attacked by Pirates and robbed of all her precious cargo."

"Oh Boy!" exclaimed Billy. "You mean you really saw the Pirates climb up rope ladders with knives in their teeth and fight the Captain and crew?"

"That must have been exciting," he continued, "but did you see what they did with all the treasure they took from the ship?"

"I sure did," answered the Turtle. "Now let me continue. In the bloody fight to capture the Galleon she was almost blown apart by cannon fire and was ready to sink, so the Pirates unloaded her treasure into small boats and took it to shore. The gold, silver and jewels were put into bags and buried in a coral cave on a sandy beach."

Billy listened breathlessly. "Go on with the story, Sea Turtle. Maybe you know where they buried the treasure out of the chest I found empty today."

"That's the rest of the story, Billy," answered the Turtle. "I know where the treasure from the Galleon is hidden, and I shall tell you where to find it."

"G-O-L-L-Y! Sounds too good to be true."

"You'll see," answered the old Green Sea Turtle. "Now listen carefully. There's a small coral island covered with palm trees, a short distance from your father's boat. You'll know this island because the sand on the shore is pink and hard and slopes gradually into the bright blue water."

"Now, Billy, I am going to this very island today, to lay my eggs. On my way to this secluded spot, I will make a cross with my flippers on the hard smooth sand. This cross will show you the spot where the Pirates buried the treasure. Now, don't forget, I will leave a cross with my flippers."

And with these words, the old Green Sea Turtle disappeared in a mist of deep blue water.

It seemed only a moment before Billy felt the hard deck of his boat under him. The air felt dry and brittle. The sun burned hot on his back, and he wished for the cool of the underseas world.

Then far off in the distance, Billy heard a voice calling: "Billy, Billy, it's almost supper time. What have you been doing all afternoon? Day-dreaming again about 'treasures under the sea,' I'll wager!"

"No! No! Dad, you're wrong. I've had a real adventure, way down under the sea. It was wonderful! I met all the fishes and I found an old Galleon and ..."

"Goodness me! What are you talking about? Come on, Billy, snap out of it."

"But Dad, it's true! It was a real adventure and the old Green Sea Turtle told me the secret, that nobody else in the whole wide world knows, nobody but me."

"Green Sea Turtles! Secret! What kind of a secret?"

"Treasure, treasure buried a long time ago by the Pirates," answered Billy importantly.

"Nonsense, what's all this silly talk? You must be ill."

"Please, it won't hurt just to look. Will it? Let's sail over to the small island with the pink sandy shore, please, Dad."

"All right, I may as well get this over with, so that you won't pester me about treasure hunting anymore."

As they reached the island and went ashore, Billy's Dad said: "I suppose the wise old Sea Turtle told you just how to start looking on a beach for hidden treasure?"

"Yes, that's exactly what she did. She promised to make a cross with her flippers right over the spot where the treasure is buried. That's the big secret."

"Um, seeing is believing. You had better start looking for that flipper cross."

Up and down the beach went Billy. He searched and searched and looked and looked, and was afraid the sun would go down and the tide come in before he found the cross left by the Turtle.

Finally running up to a new part of the beach, Billy called excitedly, "Quick, quick, here it is! Here it is! Here's the cross the Turtle made with her flippers. Good old Sea Turtle. I knew she wouldn't disappoint me. Come on, let's dig, right here."

So — Billy and his Father dug down into the hard sand, and in a small coral cave they found the buried treasure left there by the pirates, hundreds of years ago.

As Billy tugged and pulled on one of the encrusted bags, the rotten cloth broke and there spread before their startled eyes, gold and silver coins, rubies, jade and pearls.

Billy's Father looked at the treasure in wonderment and said: "Your story, Son, about exploring under the sea … talking to fish and such … was hard to believe but —"

"I know," answered Billy with a delighted grin. "It still seems almost like a dream — maybe it was — but the treasure is real and can make a lot of dreams *come true!*"

END